MW00441031

~~Damsel~~ Dude in Distress

A short story from the NYT bestselling author of the SHACKING UP series about a road trip that started with a broken-down car and ended with a questionable motel, an indoor campout and a set of Kama Sutra sheets.

Nevah

I thought I was helping a damsel in distress.

Turns out my damsel was actually a hot guy with rock solid forearms, blue eyes reminiscent of an oasis in a desert, and some seriously bad luck.

Lawson

My day started with a bang.

The kind that left me stranded at the side of the road in the middle of the desert.

At least until a knight in shining armor shows up in a rusted-out convertible and saves the day. Said knight also happens to be a car savvy woman with legs for days, and a penchant for adventure.

Praise for Helena Hunting's Novels

"Nothing hits me in the feels like a Helena Hunting romance!"

—*USA Today* bestselling author Melanie Harlow on *A Lie for a Lie*

"Helena Hunting delivers a smart, funny, emotional story that grabs you from page one."

—*Wall Street Journal* bestselling author Ilsa Madden-Mills on *A Lie for a Lie*

"A sexy, heartwarming read!"

—*New York Times* bestselling author Elle Kennedy on *A Lie for a Lie*

"*A Favor for a Favor* is now my favorite hockey book of Helena's! I loved how real the characters were. I loved the build of their friendship. It's my favorite trope, and Helena did it superbly! A huge recommend from me. Also, it was really funny too. *wink wink*"

—*New York Times* bestselling author Tijan

"Stevie and Bishop are just as funny and hot as you've come to expect from Helena Hunting! Grab a pizza and crack it open because you will not want to miss the steamy shenanigans."

—*USA Today* bestselling author Sarina Bowen on *A Favor for a Favor*

"A thoroughly delicious read."

—*USA Today* bestselling author L. J. Shen on *Kiss My Cupcake*

Dude in Distress is a work of fiction. Names, characters, places, and incidents are all products of the author's twisted imagination and are used fictitiously. Any resemblance to actual events, locals, or persons, living or dead, is entirely coincidental.

DUDE
in
DISTRESS

NEW YORK TIMES BESTSELLING AUTHOR
HELENA HUNTING

INTERSTATE 1

Roadside Attraction

NEVAH

"I'M ON MY way to you. Other than Cactus Candy, is there anything else you need me to pick up?" I use my knee to control the steering wheel and pull my hair into a ponytail. It's a gorgeous day and I want to drive with the top down as soon as I'm finished talking to my sister. Wind and phone conversations are not a winning combination.

The body of my 1959 Cadillac Eldorado needs serious TLC, and the interior is worn and dated, but any car lover knows those things can be fixed. It's what's under the hood that really counts.

Although, I will say that having AC on a drive through the desert is essential, and the one thing I made sure was in working order. No one likes underboob sweat on a cross-country road trip.

I stroke the steering wheel with real affection. I have big plans for this car, and when I'm done restoring her, she's going to be gorgeous.

I plan to bring this beauty into the twenty-first century with a top-of-the-line, state-of-the-art sound system, so I don't have to worry about things like being hands-free and not having access to my favorite road trip playlists. For the time being, my portable speaker will have to suffice.

"I'm so jealous that you're driving here." My younger sister's wistful tone makes me smile.

"Must be hard to travel the world by private jet," I tease.

My Vegas born and bred sister is married to Griffin Mills, heir to a multi-billion dollar hotel empire. We grew up living a very middle-class existence. Cosy, who is two years my junior, has always been a bit on the nomadic side, traveling as far as her beat-up cars would allow, until she met Griffin and they fell hopelessly in love with each other.

They're a totally unlikely pair from completely different backgrounds and worlds, but they work. It gives me hope that I'll find my soulmate one day. Maybe. If I can stop being attracted to the wrong kind of guy.

"I'm not going to complain about comfortable travel, but I miss road trips. We need to take one before Griffin knocks me up."

"Amen to that, sister. I assume if you're bringing it up, it means that's high on his list of priorities."

"He's been sending me links to baby name sites. He's also marked my fertile days on the calendar for the next six months." I can't tell if Cosy is amused or irritated by this. Probably the former over the latter.

"You're not even thirty."

"Yeah, but he's closing in on forty and he'd like to be

done with teenagers by the time he's sixty."

"I can see the validity in that."

Griffin Mills is a very type A, yet slightly impulsive guy. When he's in, he's all in, which is how he is with Cosy. He doesn't half-ass anything about their relationship. It's part of the reason I'm driving to Colorado to celebrate her birthday, along with what I'm suspecting will be about two hundred other people. And that's a conservative estimate.

Cosy loves Colorado and live concerts, and her favorite band just happens to be playing at the Red Rocks Amphitheatre this weekend. What's even more impressive is that Griffin somehow managed to plan this event far enough in advance (probably before he even proposed to her) and secured the band and the amphitheatre for a private concert—Cosy happens to be unaware of this fact.

I don't even want to consider how much money he spent on this, or what Cosy is going to say about it when she finds out. Cosy has always been very practical with money and extremely thrifty. Much better at financial management than I've ever been.

I'm not proud to admit that for a number of years I dated highly emotionally unavailable men who showered me with gifts and provided me with a shallow, empty, but comfortable existence.

So when my very practical, bargain-shopping, somewhat relationship averse younger sister ended up with a guy almost eleven years older than her with enough money to buy several small countries, I was surprised. I was also appropriately wary due to my own experiences with older, wealthy men, although I did cash in on his desperation a few times when he screwed things up with Cosy in the beginning.

I've matured a lot since then.

Okay, I've matured a little.

And I'm still working on making better choices with men, hence the reason I've spent the better part of the past year on self-improvement. Which also means I've been on a lengthy dating hiatus. My lady parts haven't seen action in so long that I almost feel like a born-again virgin.

I'm equal parts excited and nervous about this party. The Mills family knows how to throw a shindig. There will also be an inordinate number of insanely financially well-endowed dudes there. I'm going to do my best not to fall off the wagon and get involved with one of them. Not even just a fling.

Well . . . maybe a fling wouldn't hurt. Get back on the bike once to make sure I haven't forgotten how to ride.

"Anyway, enough about baby names and me getting knocked up. Do you think you'll be here in time for dinner? We're planning to have a campout. Griffin even set up the Airstream and there are yurts and everything!" I imagine Cosy bouncing on her toes with excitement.

I've seen Griffin's Airstream. It's nicer than the apartment Cosy and I used to live in back when she first met him. And close to the same size.

I glance at my phone, which is set in a mount on the dash. "According to the map, I'll be there in nine hours and seventeen minutes, but that's based on me driving the actual speed limit, so there's a good chance I'll be there sooner than that."

"Just don't get a speeding ticket."

"I've talked my way out of the last three, so don't you worry, little sister." I take my foot off the gas, though, because there's a car on the shoulder up ahead, and while I'm sure I can get myself out of another ticket if I need to, I'd rather avoid the delay.

I'm currently on an open stretch, having just passed the Arizona-Utah border. The road before me is flat and straight, with the desert spanning on both sides, not a cloud in the sky, and the sun is beating down, hot and bright. I adjust my sunglasses, slowing a little more as I approach the car.

It's old, definitely a classic. Those happen to be my kryptonite. When I moved to New York to be closer to my sister, I managed to score a really cool job restoring classic cars at a very exclusive body shop.

My recent trip to Vegas was spent checking out a couple of options for one of the shop's very regular clients. I'm being paid to drive across the country and tell him whether or not I think it's worth it to purchase and restore the car.

Obviously, I'm going to use the opportunity to check out a few more on the way home, and make a stop in Colorado for the weekend to hang out with my sister on her birthday.

I let out a low whistle and slow even further as I drive by the beautiful car that's apparently experiencing some engine trouble based on the propped up hood. "Oh man."

"Oh man, what?" Cosy asks.

"I just passed a 1969 Alfa Romeo Spider." I glance in the rearview mirror, noting long blonde wavy hair.

"Uh, I'm guessing that's a car and not an actual spider."

"Ha-ha. It's not just *any* car, Cosy. It's one of the top ten convertibles of all time."

"I'm taking it that's a big deal."

"It is if you know anything about cars." I glance in the mirror again, the car turning into a pinprick.

The road ahead of me is empty, not another car in sight. It's only nine-thirty and the temperature is already registering in the high eighties. It's only going to get hotter and there isn't a gas station within a five-mile radius.

I'd hate to leave a fellow woman stranded in the sweltering desert with a broken-down car. I've been that woman before. Thankfully, I know how to fix cars and I also know self-defense, two skills not all women possess, but probably should.

I take my foot off the gas and drop to the shoulder. Giving myself enough room to pull a U-turn, I spin the wheel all the way to the left and hit the gas. Gravel and sand spray across the road and my back end fishtails before the tires hit the pavement again with a screech.

"What the hell was that?" Cosy shrieks.

"I'm going back to help."

"Whoa, what? Aren't you in the middle of the desert right now?" The sound of things dropping filters through the speaker. "You are totally in the middle of the desert right now! Oh my God! You're in Utah! I can see you on the tracking app! You are not going to stop and help some random person on the side of the road, Nevah! What if it's a trick? What if they kidnap you and stuff you in the trunk and you end up in some polygamist compound?"

"I'm not going to end up in a polygamist compound, Cosy. It's a woman. Alone. And there is literally no room in that trunk for a body, at least as long as it's in one piece. I can't leave her out here without stopping to see if I can help. I'm almost at the car. I'll ring you back in ten." I end the call in the middle of her screaming at me not to hang up.

I check my rearview mirror before I cross the yellow line and pull onto the shoulder facing oncoming traffic.

The blonde lady bangs her head on the roof of the car as she tries to look over her shoulder.

That is when I realize the blonde lady isn't a lady at all. She's a dude.

So much for helping a damsel in distress.

Miss Ratchet

LAWSON

"SONOFA—" I RUB the back of my head and duck out from under the hood of my awesome, but crappy new car.

Awesome because it's a classic, and it's damn well beautiful. Crappy because as sexy as it is, it spluttered and coughed and stopped moving, so now I'm stuck in the middle of the desert sweating my balls off.

I don't even know why I bothered checking under the hood. It's not as though I know what to look for. I've changed my oil before, once, when I was a teenager, and I filled my windshield washer fluid last year, but otherwise, professionals always deal with my cars.

The woman in the shitbox convertible calls out an apology. I shield my eyes, the glare of the sun reflecting off her windshield, blinding me.

"You need some help?" She opens the driver's side door of her dusty, rusted out Caddy. It boasts a Nevada license plate.

One of her sandal clad feet hits the ground. Her toenails are painted hot pink. Her legs are cut off at the ankle by the door as she steps out of the car.

"Looks like you're having a little trouble with your baby." She uses her hip to close the door and I get a full view of my potential knightess in rusted steel and chrome.

Holy shit.

This woman's body is the thing wet dreams are made of. Her legs go on forever, long, toned, and tanned, and they're encased in a pair of denim shorts that ride high on her thighs. Three inches of equally tanned and toned stomach peek out from under the hem of her cropped tank, which has the letters *STW* stamped across her chest along with a set of cherries over her right boob.

She's wearing a baseball cap that casts a shadow over her face, and a huge pair of sunglasses.

"Hello! Everything okay there?" She runs her finger along the hood of her car, stopping when she reaches the grill.

I realize I'm gawking. "Oh, uh, yeah, I mean, no. My car broke down." I thumb over my shoulder at the propped up hood.

"Yeah, I kinda figured." One side of her mouth tips up in an amused smile. "Any idea what's wrong?"

I rub my beard and give my head a shake. "Uh, not really? And I can't get a signal, so calling a tow is tough."

"Yeah, the reception out here can be spotty depending on your carrier." She tucks a thumb into her pocket and tips her chin up. "Want me to have a look?"

I can't imagine what she's going to be able to do for me, but she's offering assistance and she's got a rockin' body, so I figure why not let her check under my hood? That way I can appreciate her very nice legs without coming across as a leering jerk.

"Sure." I shrug and step aside.

It's hotter than a sauna out here and windy, so my hair is blowing all over the place. I gather it up and use the hair tie wrapped around my wrist to secure in a topknot. Sweat trickles down my spine and my balls are sticking to the inside of my thigh. Commando is probably not the way to go in the desert.

She takes a few tentative steps closer. "I'm Nevah."

"Never?" I'm struck by a strange sense of déjà vu.

Up close I can see that she has a delicate jawline and full lips. Her long, dark hair is pulled back into a ponytail and threaded through the snapback of her ball cap. She has a dainty nose and high cheekbones, and for some reason, she seems familiar.

She grins. "Not quite. It's haven spelled backwards, but pronounced like neva eva."

"Were your parents fans of En Vogue or something?" I want to punch myself in my nuts for asking that.

Especially when she arches a brow. "If you start singing that song, I'm getting back in my car."

"Sorry. That was bad. And I can't sing, so I will definitely not offend you further by doing something so heinously disrespectful." I extend a hand. "I'm Lawson."

She glances down at my grease-streaked hand, brow furrowed. "Lawson? Is that your first name or last name?"

"First." I make a fist. "My hands are disgusting. Bump instead?"

"I'm about to get myself dirty, so I'm not really worried about it." She slips her fingers into my palm. I instantly regret it because mine is damp and hers is not. Her grip is also incredibly firm. "Also, I thought you were a woman when I first drove by, so on the off chance you're a psychopath lunatic surfer dude, I should inform you that I've taken self-defense classes and I can debilitate you with one move. I also have mace, and I can break your knees with a tire iron, if necessary." She releases my hand.

"Right. Uh, okay. Well, I'm not a psychopath lunatic surfer and I've never taken self-defense classes, so I feel like you've got a leg up on me. Also, I don't have mace, so if *you* happen to be a lunatic, it looks like there's a chance I'll end up baking to death in the sun." *Why the hell does she look so familiar?*

She drags her hand down her face to cover her grimace. "Sorry, I watched the *Don't Fuck with Cats* documentary last week. It freaked me out to think that Canadians could be serial killers, you know? Makes you wonder if they tell you they're sorry while they're lopping off your head."

"Dude! I watched that last week, too! I'm supposed to go up to Canada next month. Now I feel like I might need those self-defense lessons you're talking about and maybe the mace, too. Scared the shit right out of me. Not literally, of course, just figuratively."

"I love Netflix, but those freaking documentaries always call my name late at night. It's never a good idea, and yet I do it every time." She turns her attention to my car and ducks under the hood.

"I hear you on that." I try not to watch a lot of TV in the evening; otherwise, I find myself binging series and then I sleep until noon and fuck half my day away.

She makes another face and whistles. "I hope you weren't planning to drive this baby up to Canada.

She's gonna need a lot of work before she's ready to be ridden hard, aren't you, sweetheart?" She strokes along the fender, the same way I would caress a lover during foreplay.

Also, I'm not sure if I actually heard those words come out of her mouth or I've just been standing in the sun too long. Maybe she's not even real. She could be a mirage that my mind has conjured up. I could be lying on the ground right now, halfway to dead and not even know it.

She looks up at me, her ponytail swishing across her shoulder, and pushes her sunglasses up. For the first time, I get a look at her eyes. They're a shade of blue that reminds me of the beach. Cool and fresh and inviting. I think I might be thirsty.

"Lawson?"

"Huh?"

"How long have you been stranded out here?"

I consider raising my arm to do a sniff test, but I've already offended her with the En Vogue reference, and she's likened me to a Canadian serial killer. I'm thinking I don't want to do anything else she might consider distasteful or she'll use those self-defense skills. Unless she's an actual mirage, in which case the point is moot.

Still, on the off chance she's real, I should try to act somewhat normal. "Um, I'm not sure, but I'm pretty sweaty, so I'm going to say it's been a while. Why?"

"Because I called your name four times before you responded."

"Oh, sorry." I rub the back of my neck and go with honesty. "I was contemplating whether or not you were a hallucination. It would be just like my subconscious to conjure up a gorgeous woman who actually knows how to fix cars."

She chuckles and shakes her head. "You're something else, Lawson." She straightens and grabs the edge of the hood. "So I have some good news and some bad news. Which would you like first?"

"I guess the bad?"

"All of your spark plugs are shot. I'm surprised this girl is running at all. You also have a crack in your radiator, and I think you're leaking oil, but I'd have to get under her to be sure, and I don't have the equipment to do that here."

I rub the back of my neck again. "There's some good news in there?"

"I have a friend about fifteen miles down the road in Utah who owns a garage. I can call a tow and we can take your girl there, see what can be done to get her back on the road."

"Shit. Well, I guess that's what I get for buying a car without having it safetied first."

"How long ago did you buy it?"

"Yesterday. I took it for a spin and it ran just fine. I guess this explains why it seemed like a sweet deal." I saw the car parked on some old man's front lawn and couldn't resist stopping. Within hours, I'd bought the car and left my rental behind.

"How long was the spin you took it for?"

"Twenty minutes, give or take."

She glances at the California plates. "You drove that from California all the way here?"

"Yeah."

"How far are you planning to go?"

"Long Island."

Her eyebrows pop. "Did you tell the guy who sold

you the car that you're driving all the way across the country?"

"Uh, I didn't really think it was relevant?" Although, I suppose I should've asked for more clarification, but it's a cool car, and it seemed like a good deal. I also didn't feel like spending hours at an airport when I could enjoy the open road instead. Two states later, and the road trip vibe is definitely wearing off.

"Right, okay. Well, I'm not sure you're gonna make it that far without some serious surgery. I'll call my friend, then?"

That's not what I want to hear, but frying in the sun isn't a viable option. "That'd be great, yeah, thanks."

She digs her phone out of her back pocket, punches a bunch of buttons, and brings it to her ear. "Hey, Bear, how's it going?"

She has a friend named *Bear*? I don't know what to make of her, and I honestly wish I could figure out why I feel like I've met her before. It seems impossible what with her Nevada plates.

Two minutes later, she tosses her phone into her car. "My friend's sending a tow out. Should be here in about twenty."

"Great. Thanks a lot." I swipe my arm across my forehead. I could really use a shower, or a pool, or some air conditioning.

After about thirty seconds of silence, in which we both look around uncomfortably, she thumbs over her shoulder. "You wanna sit in my car while we wait? I'm sweating my tits off, so I gotta imagine it can't be all that nice for you either."

"Uh, that'd be great. Thanks. I'm just gonna grab a bottle of water."

"Good plan. It's hot enough to fry a steak out here."

I walk around the side of my car and lean over to grab the bottle of water I left in the center console. It has to be a full twenty degrees hotter inside the car than it is outside. "Fuck," I mutter when I remember that there are freaking Amalie dolls strapped into the passenger seat.

My dad made an empire out of dolls that look like my younger sister. At least they started out looking like her. She's essentially a much more proportional human version of a Barbie doll. Now they come with every conceivable hair color and skin tone possible.

You can have them made to look exactly like your kid. We have girl and boy dolls with customized clothing options. There's even an interactive app. I'm in charge of the social media for the dolls, which means I spend a lot of time dressing them up and posing them for pictures.

It sounds pretty lame.

Which is why I dabble in real estate on the side. And buying classic cars on a whim. Based on how that's going so far, I think I'll stick with real estate.

I'm also aware that it looks really fucking weird to have a couple of dolls meant for six year olds riding shotgun in my car. I unbuckle the seat belt, toss them in the back, and shrug out of my super sweaty shirt. I grab my spare, which is draped over the back of the passenger seat, and the bottle of water.

I shrug into my dry shirt and fasten a single button. I can't believe how freaking hot it is. It's like living on the underside of a nut sack in a sauna.

My flip-flops slap the pavement, sticking a little with each step, as if they're halfway to melting. I slide into the passenger seat of Nevah's car and sigh when a blast of cold air hits my sweaty face and chest.

"Did the guy who sold you his car also sell you that shirt?" Nevah's eyebrows lift above her sunglasses.

I run a hand down the patterned fabric. It's an ocean blue Hawaiian print with penguins surfing waves. It's meant to go with our Amalie Summer Beach campaign. The bright colors are eye-catching and do well in Instagram photos. "If I say no, are you going to make a comment about ransacking my grandfather's closet?"

"I don't have to anymore since you just did." She grabs a water bottle from the backseat, unscrews the cap, and drains the entire thing in three long swallows.

"Wow. You must kick some serious ass at keg stand challenges."

"It was probably my favorite subject in college, and consequently the reason I never graduated." She waves a hand around in the air, as if she's erasing her words. "Anyway, Lawson, tell me why you're driving across the country if you're not on the run?"

"Uh, well, I had some business in California I had to take care of and I have a couple of stops on the way back home to Long Island, so I figured instead of flying I'd buy a car and bring it back home and fix it up."

"Just like that, huh?"

"Just like that. Although I'm starting to think my plan is flawed."

She holds her fingers half an inch apart. "Maybe a little."

We make small talk while we wait for the tow truck to show up and I keep trying to figure out why she's so damn familiar.

When the tow arrives, I assume she's going to leave, but instead, she offers to follow the tow truck to the garage.

"You've already gone out of your way to help me, I can just ride in the truck." I motion to the burly, pot-bellied chain-smoking man currently giving us an excellent view of his ass crack as he secures my beautiful, broken car. Nevah leans over and pops the glove box. She grabs a small baggie, stuffs it into her back pocket, and calls out, "You bring your girl with you, Kenny?"

"Sure did, Nev," he shouts back.

"You mind if I say hi?"

"Go for it."

Nevah struts over to the passenger side of the tow truck, glancing briefly over her shoulder at me, while smirking. She whistles and calls out, "Princess, you keeping Kenny in line?" A giant Bull Mastiff's head pokes out of the passenger side window, tongue lolling as soon as the dog spots Nevah. She barks once and a long string of drool drips slowly from her jowls to the ground.

Nevah pulls the baggie from her back pocket, retrieves a treat, and places it carefully on the end of the dog's nose. Princess waits until she's given the signal before she flips the treat off her nose and catches it with her giant tongue.

"I think you're better off riding with me. Princess isn't big on sharing her seat." Nevah gives me a wink.

I stand awkwardly off to the side while she and Kenny discuss who should take me to the garage. He seems concerned about her welfare. I'm more concerned about Princess taking a bite out of me should I have to ride in Kenny's truck. Or the possibility that I'm being duped and these two are black market organ thieves and they're driving me to my demise. I really hope not.

INTERSTATE
3

Six Degrees

NEVAH

KENNY IS NOT pleased about my surfer friend Lawson riding with me. I assure him I'll be fine and we'll be right behind his truck.

The second I get into the car my phone lights up with a call. It's definitely been more than ten minutes since I hung up on Cosy.

"Shit. That's my sister. She's probably losing her mind."

I answer the call and Cosy's voice blares through the speaker in the backseat. "Ten fucking minutes, you said, Nevah. Ten minutes! I can see that you're still in the same damn place! What the hell is going on?"

"Sorry, the whole helping out someone in need is taking a little longer than I expected." I disconnect the phone from the speaker so our conversation is no longer public.

"Wait, hold on. Are you still dealing with that lady

and her broken-down car?"

"Uh, yeah, except that lady is actually a dude."

"Are you fucking kidding me?" Her voice is so loud I cringe away from the phone. Based on Lawson's uncomfortable expression, he also hears her.

"I am, in fact, not fucking kidding you at all. And he's harmless. He has a manbun and he's wearing a Hawaiian shirt and flip-flops. Nothing about him screams serial killer. Isn't that right?" I give Lawson a pointed look. I cannot figure out what the deal is with this guy. I feel like I've seen him before. Maybe because he looks like every single surfer dude ever cast in a movie?

He shakes his head. "Definitely not a serial killer, unless you count actual edible cereal. I can kill a box of that for breakfast no problem."

I roll my eyes. "See, Cosy? He's perfectly harmless."

"Why the hell is he still with you?"

"Because his car is fucked and I'm taking him to Bear's garage to see what the deal is. I couldn't leave him there." I don't have much hope for Lawson's ride. It's pretty, but I have a feeling it needs some serious love before it's back on the road.

"You know some guy named Bear in Utah?" Cosy sounds appalled.

"Barry Fisher, from high school. Had a full beard by the time he hit junior year. Played football. You remember him?"

"Oh! Yeah. What's he doing in Utah?"

"Running a garage."

"Obviously." I can practically hear her eye roll. "Still, having some random guy you don't know in your car is grounds for me to freak out. I vote you stay on the phone with me until you reach the garage. Do you even know his name?"

"It's Lawson. Even his name sounds harmless." I wink at my passenger.

"Do you happen to have a last name to go with the first name?" Cosy asks.

"My sister would like to know what your last name is." I hold the phone in his direction.

He leans closer so he can speak directly into it like a mic. "Whitfield. Lawson Whitfield."

"Thanks. Did you catch that?" I ask my sister.

"Lawson *Whitfield*?" Cosy is back to high-pitch shrieking.

"I believe so, yes."

"Ask him if he has any brothers or sisters."

"Do you want to ask him yourself?"

"Just do it." Cosy can be bossy and overprotective for a little sister.

"Lawson, do you have any siblings?"

"Yeah, two, a sister and a brother." I bet he regrets buying that car for more reasons than it just breaking down.

"Ask him if his sister's name is Amalie."

"You mean Sexy Lexy's wife?" Amalie, otherwise known as Amie, pronounced Ah-me, is married to Griffin's brother Lexington, aka Lex, or Sexy Lexy as we like to call him. Cosy's husband is a big dude, but his younger brother looks like some kind of sexy Spartan warrior. All of the Mills brothers are mountains of hot men, actually. Unfortunately, they're all taken.

"Just ask him!" Cosy demands.

"Is your sister's name Amalie?"

"Uh, yeah. How would you know that?" His fingers inch along the armrest, as if he's prepared to do a tuck and roll out of the car.

"My sister, Cosy, is married to Griffin Mills, Lex's older brother," I tell him. "I think that makes your sister and my sister sisters-in-law?" It's more of a question than an actual statement, because I'm mentally trying to figure out if this is true, and how wild it is that I managed to find him in the middle of a freaking desert.

Lawson's eyes flare. "No shit. I thought you looked familiar!"

"Same. We must've been at the same event at some point in the past couple of years." It explains why it felt like I knew him. It also makes me feel a little better about having some not-so-random hot dude in my car.

I end the call with my sister, who is no longer worried about me ending up dismembered, since apparently Lawson and I know each other, however indirectly.

"How crazy is this! I can't believe our sisters are in-laws."

"Me neither, to be honest. I mean, what are the chances?" Lawson rubs his scruffy chin.

"Slim to freaking none, I would think."

We pull into the garage and I'm greeted with enthusiasm and a bone-crushing hug from Bear, who I haven't seen in more than a year. I introduce him to Lawson, and explain that we actually know each other, which seems to put Kenny at ease. Sort of. He's still mumbling about the pretty boy and how I love picking up strays. He's not wrong about Lawson being pretty.

Bear and Kenny get the car up on one of the lifts and it takes about thirty seconds to come to the conclusion that as nice as the car looks, it's not drivable. Turns out, I was right about the oil leak and the radiator.

"So how long before I can get back on the road?"

Lawson asks.

"Probably a few weeks, depending on how long it takes to order in the parts since it's a classic and all," Bear says.

Lawson laces his hands behind his head. "Well, shit. I'm supposed to be in Colorado tomorrow night."

I slap the side of his car, realization finally dawning. "Hold on, are you going to Cosy's party?"

"The Mills birthday bash thing?"

"Yeah."

"That was my plan until my car broke down."

"I'm heading there now, so you might as well ride with me. Road trips are way more fun with a sidekick, anyway."

Lawson nods his agreement. "Definitely way more fun."

Looks like my trip to Colorado just got a whole lot more interesting.

INTERSTATE
4

Another Detour

LAWSON

"I CANNOT BELIEVE I blew a tire. What the hell was that random piece of wood doing in the middle of the freaking road?" Nevah throws her hands in the air and kicks the deflated rubber. "I'm gonna have to put the spare on."

"Can you drive all the way to Colorado Springs on a spare?" I have no idea, so it's an honest question.

"Depends on the car. Most of the time you can go a hundred miles or so on a spare, but we're a lot farther out than that, and I don't really want to risk bending the frame on this baby." She pats her car affectionately. "We'll get the spare on and see how far we can go before we hit a garage."

We've made it most of the way through Utah. Over the past several hours, I've learned a lot about Nevah.

As it turns out, we've attended more than one social gathering together. In fact, I'm fairly certain I had plans to hit on her while I was drunk, but my sister intervened before I could make a complete ass out of myself.

Truth be told, I'm not very good at the whole relationship thing. Or talking to women in general. I'm awesome at social media and creating a brand and flirting on line. I'm also adept at picking up women at bars because there isn't a whole lot of talking involved. It's not that I don't want to have conversations with women; it's more that my job is weird, my family is well known, and I'm slightly socially awkward—see the En Vogue comment for reference.

I now know that Nevah took public relations, business, and plumbing in college and decided none of them were the right fit. She's always been fascinated with cars. While other girls were playing with Barbies, she was playing with Barbie's corvette and spray-painting it black to make it cooler.

She learned how to jump-start a car when she was sixteen while hanging out with some less than savory characters, one of which happened to be Barry, aka Bear. She's narrowly escaped a criminal record more than once, and has a long history of dating jerks. She didn't go into much detail about that, other than to say most of the time she liked their cars better than she liked the guys who were driving them.

She pops the trunk and I move my suitcase out of the way. One of the dolls rolls out from under my shirt. It's a brown-haired Amalie doll with a pretty sweet tan, wearing a two-piece halter tank that somewhat matches my current shirt.

She glances from me to the doll and back again.

"It's not what you think," I blurt, which obviously makes it sound like exactly what she thinks, even though

I can't be sure what exactly that is.

Grown men who tote around kids' dolls incite a lot of questions.

She cocks a brow. "So you don't have a doll with a bathing suit that matches your shirt in my trunk?"

"It's the family business. Amalie dolls. I was in California working with a company that uses all recycled plastics and materials to make dolls and their clothes," I explain.

"Amalie dolls? Holy crap! Amalie is your sister. Wow! I'm the slowest person ever. I can't believe I didn't make the connection." She picks up the plastic doll and hugs it to her chest. "I wanted one so bad when I was a kid, but my parents said they were too expensive."

"You can have that one if you want." I'm thankful that she knows what the fuck I'm talking about and doesn't think I'm just some random weirdo with a doll fetish. I mean, I have a little too much fun posing them for photo shoots, but not in a creepy way, just in an *if I have to pose dolls for photo shoots as a grown man, I might as well have some fun with it* way.

"Oh no, I couldn't. I'm way too old to play with dolls." She continues to hug it and stroke its hair.

"Are you really, though?" I point to myself. "My job is to literally play with those dolls." As soon as those words are out of my mouth, I wish I could stuff them back in with a hot fiery poker. Thankfully, she doesn't mace me and run.

"Hmm, you make a good point." She chuckles and sets the doll back in the trunk, carefully, though, and frees the spare tire. I offer to help, but mostly it's just me handing her things and trying to stay out of the way while she changes the flat.

The sun is starting to creep toward the horizon, and by the time we make it to the next town, it's nearing six, and the only garage in town closed an hour ago.

Nevah drops her head against the rest and blows out a breath. "I don't think we're making it to Colorado tonight, Lawson."

"You're probably right, unless you want to resort to hitchhiking."

"I'm going to say no thanks to that." Nevah drums on the steering wheel. "There was a motel about a mile back. Should we see about getting a couple of rooms for the night?"

"WHAT DO YOU mean there's only one room left?" Nevah taps her hot pink nails on the pitted counter. There's a chip in the index one and grease lines her cuticles. For some reason, I find that sexy. Possibly because her ability to change tires saved us from either having to hike the ten miles into town or wait until yet another tow truck came to pick us up.

"I'm sorry, ma'am, but the sheriff's daughter is getting married this weekend and all the other rooms are rented out 'cause the whole family is in town. Lots of aunts and uncles." The teenager, whose nametag reads Lucifer, gives her an apologetic half-smile. "Grand Junction is about thirty miles down the road. They'll surely have two rooms. They even have a Double Tree there, real nice and swanky. Kinda expensive, though."

Nevah raps on the counter a couple more times. "How do you feel about sleeping together?"

My eyebrows pop and the kid chokes on a sip of his Mountain Dew.

"I mean in the same room." She rolls her eyes "Boys. So predictable."

"If you're okay with it, I'm okay with it." I'm actually more than okay with it, but I'm trying not to come across as douchey, since there's been a lot of potential for that over the course of this day.

"We can always hit up a church on Sunday if we're feeling guilty about it," Nevah mutters. "Okay, we'll take the room." She digs around in her purse for her wallet, which gives me the opportunity to be faster on the credit card draw.

The motel is so old and out-of-date that they have to use one of those manual credit card machines. And the cash register looks like it was resurrected from the 1950s. The kid gives us a key on an actual keychain with the phrase *He's always watching* stamped on it.

"There's a pool in the back and it's open until ten, and ice machines are closest to rooms twenty-five and one. The vending machines only take quarters, but they're open all night," Lucifer says this in monotone, as if it's something he's rehearsed and still has trouble remembering.

"Great, thanks." Nevah's tone implies she thinks this is anything but great.

"Is there anywhere we can grab a bite to eat, or a beer?" I ask before we head to our room. Which we're sleeping in. Together.

"Oh, yes!" Lucifer perks right up. "There's a bar about a five-minute walk down the road called the Pickled Onion and they serve food and beer until midnight. And there's a 7-Eleven just down the street. The have really great taquitos and they sell beer, too."

"Fantastic. You have yourself a great night, Lucifer."

"You too. Enjoy your stay!" he calls after us.

Nevah parks the car in front of room twenty-five and I grab both of our bags from the trunk. It's the least I can do seeing as she's saved my ass a lot today.

She unlocks the door and steps aside to let me in, following on my heels.

"Wow. I didn't realize there were this many shades of shit brown." Nevah drops her purse onto the brown table and surveys what is a very, very brown room.

"Their commitment to shades of crap is astounding."

The carpet is a horrible yellow-brown that reminds me of baby poop, the walls are beige—although it smells like stale cigarettes and a very pungent, floral room spray in here, so there's a good chance those are nicotine stains. Even the print on the wall, which looks like it might have been cut from a calendar, consists of brown cattails. But the best, or worst part, is the shiny brown comforter with an orange geometric pattern.

I motion to the bed. "This is like being on an acid trip without even doing drugs."

"Uh, I think we have an issue." Nevah's nose wrinkles as she takes in the hideous comforter.

"You're allergic to brown polyester?"

"Ha-ha." She gives me the side-eye. "Have you noticed that there's something big missing?"

"Class? Taste? A color that isn't brown?" I'll admit, I'm used to five-star accommodations. Even in its prime this place wouldn't rank at a point-five.

"Yes, it's missing all of those things." Nevah crosses her arms. "It's also missing a second bed."

INTERSTATE 5

I See You Hanging There

NEVAH

I'VE SLEPT IN some shitty places over the course of my life. My parents are great people, but we were firmly entrenched in the low end of middle class growing up. I had a single bed until I was eighteen, and the same mattress from the time I was four until I finally moved out. Incidentally, my parents sold the house at that time and bought an RV so they could travel around the US.

We're a family of nomads. Hell, I spent a number of months sleeping on my sister's couch when I was going through a particularly rough patch that included one of my douche exes.

But this motel is another level of shitty.

Lawson rocks back on his heels. "I can sleep on the floor."

"It might actually be the more hygienic location." I pick up the corner of the comforter and rub the fabric between my fingers. "This could double as a tarp."

Lawson jams his thumbs into his pockets and rocks back on his heels. "Do you think there's a HomeGoods or even a Walmart close by where we could grab sheets? Or maybe sleeping bags and a couple of blowup mattresses?"

"Oh my God!" I grab Lawson by the lapels of his shirt. Only one button is fastened, just below the center of his chest, so his incredibly perfect six-pack abs have been gloriously on display. I've been trying not to stare at them all day. Or his nipple ring.

"Did you see a cockroach?" He makes a gagging sound.

"What? No! And I really hope I don't either. But I do have some very good news."

"Okay. I'd love some of that right about now." His eyes are such a pretty blue and they're currently locked on mine as he awaits my ray of verbal sunshine.

"I have a set of bed sheets and a comforter in my car. They're actually a gift for Cosy's birthday. I realize that sounds like a weird gift. Especially for someone married to a freaking hotel mogul billionaire who can buy her a jet if he feels like it. Which he's considered. But there's a big long story to go with the sheets, and I'll happily tell you the entire thing after we strip this down and put on fresh, fornication-free bedding."

Lawson cringes. "I was really trying not to think about that, but if I'm honest, it was the first thing that came to mind when we stepped inside this room."

I mirror his cringey face. "Same, unfortunately." I release his lapels, realizing I've been right up in his personal space. "I'll just grab the sheets from the car."

"Sounds good. And if you happen to have a hazmat suit or two, that'd be great."

"I'll see what I can do." I head back outside and grab the comforter and sheet set I had custom designed for my sister. The great thing about a Cadillac Eldorado is that the trunk is huge, so I can store a lot of crap in here. I rummage around in the recess of the trunk, practically climbing inside to get to the back in case there are things in there that I've forgotten about.

I snag the handle of Cosy's very old, very worn-out backpack. While I was in Vegas, I visited with my parents, who were there for a friend's retirement party. They're also coming to the party, but they left a couple of days early with plans to stop along the way.

I found the bag in their storage unit, along with some photo albums from our teen years, and thought Cosy might get a kick out of them. I didn't bother checking the contents of the backpack before I tossed it into the trunk, but it doesn't hurt to see what's in there.

I carry the load of stuff back into the motel room just as Lawson comes out of the bathroom, wiping his hands on his shorts while wearing a look of absolute disgust.

"I'm guessing it's pretty nasty in there." I drop the backpack and the wrapped box containing my sister's birthday gift onto the table because I don't want to contaminate anything by allowing it to touch the bed.

"I've seen nicer outhouses."

"It's that bad?" Considering Lawson's family are the creators of a doll that's been popular for a good two decades, I'll go out on a limb and assume he hasn't had to use many outhouses in his lifetime.

"Do you remember what the showers used to look like in high school locker rooms?" he asks somberly.

I nod.

"It's worse."

There isn't a whole lot of space between the bed and the ancient dresser boasting a tube TV straight out of the nineties, so we both have to turn sideways to pass each other. My chest brushes his diaphragm and my fingers skim the back of his arm, causing both of us to break out into goosebumps.

We each mutter, "Sorry," as I peek inside the bathroom. "Oh, wow."

"The wallpaper really adds a nice psychedelic touch."

"It's definitely trippy." Once again, the brown-orange theme is carried through in the bathroom. What was once a white sink is now beige with age and grime. The toilet seat lid is one of those shell numbers. The plain white plastic shower curtain has several holes in it. I peek my head in, noting the rust stains around the faucets and the very grey tint to the tub. "I think it's probably a good idea to treat this like the gym and shower with your flip-flops on."

"I would one hundred percent agree with that statement. I also think air-drying is recommended over using one of those towels." Lawson's finger appears in my peripheral vision and I follow it to the brown towels folded neatly on the vanity.

"Probably a good idea."

"Should we tackle the sheets before we brave the shower?"

"Sure."

We strip the bed down to the mattress pad and immediately wish we hadn't. I don't even want to know what the mattress looks like based on the vast number of unidentifiable stains. We debate the merits of sleeping on the floor, which had originally been a joke, and decide it's probably the safer of the two options.

Before I open the gift box containing her sheets and comforter, I open Cosy's old travel backpack. "Holy shit, Lawson! We just hit the mother lode!"

I start pulling out items. It's one of those huge backpacks that can hold an insane amount of stuff, including a two-person pop-up tent and a double-sized air mattress with pump and inflatable pillows. There are also some granola bars, but they've been expired for about two years, so unfortunately they get tossed.

Twenty minutes later, the tent is set up, the air mattress inflated, and I've unwrapped my sister's birthday present. I'm sure she'll forgive me for giving it to her used once I provide her with the photographic evidence of our less than appealing accommodations. An actual campground probably would've been a better option, but we're here now, and at least we won't have to deal with bears and woodland creatures visiting us in the night—hopefully.

I tear through the plastic and pull out the sheet set first. Lawson and I crawl back inside the tent so we can put them on the air mattress. We took turns stepping on the pump to inflate it.

He frowns as he takes one end of the fitted sheet, leaning in closer to inspect the design. "What's going on here?"

"They're Kama Sutra sheets." I grin. Prior to meeting her husband, my sister was a virgin. A twenty-two-year-old virgin who also happened to work at an adult toy store. Yes, there's a lot of irony in that.

Lawson barks out a laugh. "Holy fuck, they sure are. Where'd you get these? I want a set."

"I found them online." I also bought myself a set because they're hilarious and maybe one day I'll find my own soulmate who will want to work his way through every single position featured on these ridiculous sheets.

While we make the bed, I tell Lawson the story of how Cosy and Griffin met and eventually fell in love, despite the odds being stacked against them. He'd drawn the short straw for a bachelor party and ended up at the store where Cosy worked. She helped him check all the things off on his list, including a double-headed dildo. He'd been mortified and she'd had way more fun than was reasonable dealing with his embarrassment.

He'd come back a few weeks later to ask her out on a date. At first she'd said no, but eventually she caved, and the rest is history.

By the time we're done making the bed, I'm flushed, and not because of the exertion. Looking at endless sex positions while inside a tent with a hot guy reminds me exactly how long it's been since I've had actual sex.

"So." I prop my fists on my hips. "Based on the state of this room, I'm guessing the pool is probably not something we want to swim in unless we'd like to end up with an extra limb growing out of our foreheads."

"While extra limbs might be useful, I'm inclined to skip the pool." Lawson pulls the elastic free and his hair tumbles down, reaching his shoulders in the kind of loose, beachy waves women spend hours at a salon to achieve.

I'm still wearing a baseball cap and have been all day. I'm sure I have the worst case of hat head and my hair is extra greasy because I didn't bother washing it this morning, thinking I'd be relaxing in a Jacuzzi tub by evening.

"So showers and then check out that pub?"

"Sounds like a plan." Lawson thumbs over his shoulder. "Ladies first, of course."

I gather up my shower supplies and a change of clothes and lock myself in the bathroom. The hot water has two modes, scalding and lukewarm. Aware that I'll be sleeping beside this man tonight, on a double mattress no less, I take it upon myself to shave my legs. I don't want it to feel like he's rubbing up against burrs should we accidentally make contact under the sheets. I have no reasonable explanation for shaving the rest of my important bits, apart from the fact that it's habit. And maybe also because I have sex on the brain after staring at those sheets.

While I don't intend to jump Lawson's bones, I would also not be opposed to it. He's a good-looking guy, and despite the slew of very unfortunate events and his complete lack of car knowledge, I've enjoyed his company. We could definitely have some fun this weekend, which isn't something I've allowed myself to do in a long time.

I use the blow dryer in lieu of a towel to dry off, change into a comfy sundress, and give Lawson a turn in the shower.

"I'm just going to check out the vending machine. Any requests?" I ask as I run my brush through my wet hair.

"I'll eat just about anything, except nuts. I don't trust those from a vending machine." He shrugs out of his shirt and drapes it over the brown velour chair in the corner of the room, giving me an excellent view of his defined chest and rippling abs. His cargo shorts hang low on his hips, displaying that delicious V of muscle.

"No nuts. Got it," I echo, then bite my tongue before I say something about how much I love nuts.

On my way to the vending machine, I take a detour to

the pool, just to check it out. A sad, half-deflated beach ball floats in the green tinged water, and about half a tree's worth of leaves covers the bottom. There's also a film of algae lining the edge.

I call Cosy as I head toward the vending machines.

"Why are you still in Utah?"

Sometimes this app thing where we can see exactly where each other is at any given time is as much a curse as a blessing. "We ran into a bit of a hiccup."

"What kind of hiccup? Wait a second, are you at a motel?"

"I blew a tire and all the garages are closed until morning. I don't want to drive another four hours on a spare and risk bending the frame on Ellie, so Lawson and I are staying here for the night." I always name my cars.

"At a motel? With Lawson?"

"Yeah." I approach the ancient vending machine and rummage around in my purse for coins. The selection is unsurprisingly weak.

"In separate rooms?"

"They only had one left."

"You're in the middle of buttfuck nowhere. How are all the rooms rented out?" Her disbelief is not unwarranted.

"There's a wedding." I start shoving quarters into the slot. "Look, I need whatever intel you have on this Lawson guy. He seems nice, but you know how shitty my man radar is."

"Already looked into him. Based on Griffin's reports, he's a good guy. Kinda awkward, used to be a bit of a playboy, but seems to have settled down in the past couple of years. Might have asked about you at a party a while back. I don't know if he's relationship material, but if you're having fun with him I can give you my sisterly approval and a green light to enjoy yourself should you end up spooning tonight."

Griffin is a very stand-up guy, so his opinion is generally something I trust. "Okay. Thanks. Sister approval noted and appreciated. I'll call you in the morning when we're back on the road."

"Sounds good. Have fun and stay safe." She makes a kissy sound. "Love you!"

I end the call feeling good about my judgment as far as Lawson is concerned and go back to assessing my snack options. Funyuns and Cool Ranch Doritos, while delicious, are not ideal when sleeping in close quarters with a man I don't know that well, but find attractive. Also, Cosy's green light factors in at least a little.

I settle on a bag of plain chips and another of pretzels, even though I don't particularly love them either. I check the dates to make sure they're not expired before I also buy a package of Nibs and another of sour gummies. I only have enough quarters left for one bottle of Mountain Dew, but we can share.

"I come bearing gifts!" I shout as I shoulder my way through the door. And freeze because standing in the middle of the room with one foot in a pair of fresh cargo shorts is Lawson.

And he's commando.

Free balling.

Also, he has a peen piercing.

INTERSTATE 6

Speed Dating

LAWSON

I CHECKED TO make sure Nevah was still hitting up the vending machine before I stepped out of the bathroom. That was less than thirty seconds ago. I'm currently balanced on one leg, trying to get my foot in my shorts, but I'm wearing my flip-flops and I'm still damp post-shower, so the fabric is sticking to my skin, making the task virtually impossible.

This wouldn't be so bad if I was, say, wearing boxer briefs. But I'm not. Because I don't own underwear. I find them constrictive and an unnecessary expense. The only time I like my balls cupped is when a nice soft hand is fondling them. Preferably not my own.

"Holy wow." Nevah is standing in the middle of the open doorway carrying an armload of snacks. A bottle of soda slips from her hold, bounces off her right foot, and lands on the nasty brown carpet with a thud.

"Ow! Fuck!" Nevah drops the rest of the stuff, grabs

her toe, and hops around on one foot, face contorted in a mask of pain.

A family of four just happens to pass by our open door at exactly the same time. The mom gasps and covers her children's eyes while her own lock on my swinging junk. One of them is a teenage girl who tries to pry her mom's hand away.

I trip over my shorts and face-plant into the carpet.

"Sorry, so sorry!" Nevah shouts and slams the door in their shocked faces.

She slides down the wall, and a loud pop startles us both. Pretzels shoot across the carpet like shrapnel, and I get beaned in the forehead with a rogue piece. My cheek is currently pressed against the disgusting carpet that smells like a combination of filth and green olive juice. My legs are tangled up in my shorts, so I'm forced to flip over onto my back.

"Oh God! Get up, get up!" Nevah hobble rushes over and slides her arms under mine. I probably weigh a good sixty pounds more than she does, so I'm impressed that she manages to pull me a couple of feet toward the tent; however, the carpet has the texture of sandpaper and is highly unpleasant.

"Ahh! Stop! My balls are dragging on the carpet!" I shout. I also think I'm getting rug burn on my ass.

"Sorry! I was trying to lift you, but you're a hell of a lot heavier than I expected." She jumps back as I spring to my feet, still swinging free, bare ass on display. I yank my shorts up the rest of the way, making sure I'm tucked in before I zip up the fly and fasten the button.

Her hand is in front of her face, but there's a narrow gap between two fingers and her eyes are trained on my crotch.

"What the hell just happened?"

"Probably a lot of things I could go to prison for in this town."

Nevah snorts a laugh, which, of course, means I start laughing, too. She grabs my shoulders and sags against me, laughing so hard tears stream down her face.

"You just flashed an entire family."

"I thought I had enough time to get dressed before you got back."

She sucks in a ragged breath and tips her head up, eyes wide and suddenly serious. "Your dick is pierced."

The entire front of her body is pressed against the entire front of mine. It's giving my decorated dick a whole lot of ideas. I nod. "It is."

"So is your tongue." Her eyes are hooded and her lips part, her own tongue peeking out.

"You're correct." I sweep the steel ball across my bottom lip.

She tracks the movement and mutters something that sounds like *good idea* before she takes a step back. Her hands slide down my shoulders and over my chest. "And your nipple." She tugs on the steel ring with a devilish smirk.

"You're observant, aren't you?"

"And you're a masochist." She waggles her eyebrows. "Put a shirt on. I'm starving and I need a stiff drink."

I exhale a slow breath, willing my body to calm down. I probably should've taken care of business in the shower, but it felt skeezy to jerk off when the woman who saved my ass more than once today, who I also have to sleep beside tonight, might be on the other side of the door.

I grab a shirt from my bag and pull it over my head,

then twist my hair up, fastening it in a topknot while Nevah cleans up the exploded bag of pretzels.

"We're down a snack." She tosses it into the garbage beside the mini fridge.

"I don't like pretzels anyway."

"Me either! They're like the rejects of the snack world. Literally the last thing I would ever consider, but options were limited and I didn't feel like Cool Ranch Dorito breath was a good plan for tent sleeping."

"Very considerate of you." I reach for the doorknob, but she grabs my arm.

"Wait, let's make sure that family isn't still out there." She cracks the door and pokes her head out. Once she's sure the coast is clear, we lock up and head down the street in the direction of the bar. It's after ten and I'm starving.

The bar is exactly what I'd expect based on our accommodations: Small, dank, and lacking in ambiance. However, it's the only place open and we're both hungry, so it'll have to do. We order water and beer while we browse the menu. "I basically want to eat everything."

"Same, girl, same." I pat my growling belly.

We order greasy food and are on our second beer by the time the food arrives.

"So tell me about this." Nevah swipes her fry through her ketchup and motions toward me before biting the end off.

"Tell you about what?"

She props her chin on her fist. "You. The packaging. I'm trying to figure you out."

"The packaging?"

"You look and dress like a surfer dude."

"If I lived in California, I probably would be a surfer

dude."

"But you live in Long Island?"

"The Hamptons."

"Oooh, fancy."

"My brother and I manage a bunch of properties out there. You should come visit sometime if you're ever out that way. It's great there in the summer."

"Is this you saying you want to see me again after this weekend?" She gives me the side-eye and brings her bottle to her lips, a slight smile turning up the corners of her mouth.

"Yeah, I guess I am. I mean, we'll be sleeping together on a set of sheets covered in questionably impossible sex positions and you've already seen the goods—" I motion below the bar. "—seems like maybe we're dating already."

Nevah throws her head back and laughs. "You're ridiculous."

"But am I?" I turn so I'm facing her. "Usually a first date is coffee, or something short, right? An hour, two tops? Then you decide if you want to give the person a second shot. The next date is maybe dinner? A movie, which you can't even talk through. We've been together for twelve solid hours and we've already dealt with a broken-down car, a flat tire, and a motel that's grosser than a high school locker room. That's like what? At least three or four dates worth of time together?"

Nevah cocks a brow. "Those would be pretty fail dates."

"Obviously, actual dates with me would not include broken-down cars, flat tires, and crappy motels. What I'm saying is, we already know we're compatible, especially under pressure. Neither of us lost our cool today, other than you kicking the flat, which I think was completely warranted because that tire was an asshole. I don't know about you, but despite this day being a complete clusterfuck, I've had a lot of fun and it's been because I've had great company. Doesn't hurt that you're a smokeshow either."

"I've had a lot of fun today, too." She bites her lip and ducks her head. "It's kind of crazy that we even managed to cross paths, don't you think?"

I've thought the same thing a hundred times. "Seems a lot like fate to me."

"Do you really believe that?" Nevah regards me thoughtfully.

"Yeah, sure. Things always happen for a reason. Just like we've been at the same events before, in the same room, feet away from each other, but we've never been introduced, probably because the timing wasn't right. In fact, I know that's the case because you were at the Mills hospital fundraiser last year and I asked my sister about you."

"What did you want to know about me?"

"If you were available. I don't know if you're aware, but you're stunning. Anyway, my sister told me that I wasn't allowed to talk to you unless I was sober, which I was not at the time."

"That was probably some sage advice."

"I agree." I clink my beer against hers. "To second chances at making first impressions."

We finish our beers, pay the tab, and head back to the motel. Nevah is flirty, arm threaded through mine, cheek resting on my biceps as we navigate the uneven sidewalk. We make a stop at the 7-Eleven to load up on better snacks, including a six-pack of those powdered donuts that are equally horrible and delicious.

The motel is quiet when we return. Despite the rough start to our day, and the bad luck, this has probably been the most fun I've had with a member of the opposite sex in a long time. Generally, my relationships don't have much in the way of longevity, so the fact that I've spent an entire day with the same woman, *not* having sex, says a lot. And possibly not a lot of good things.

After we dump our treats onto the table, we stand in the middle of the room and stare at the tent for several seconds. The chill, easy vibe is suddenly rife with new tension.

"Uh, I'm going to get ready for bed." Nevah grabs her bag and disappears into the bathroom.

I really don't know what to expect tonight.

I should probably *not* expect sex. At all. Even though I'm pretty sure I would like the sex. Okay, I'm more than pretty sure. My dick, which has been in a state of semi-arousal all day long, would definitely like the sex.

I figure under these circumstances, it's probably best for me to keep my hands to myself unless otherwise requested. Especially since Nevah is basically my only way to Colorado at the moment. I also genuinely like her and I'd prefer not to mess this up.

Wanna Snuggle?

NEVAH

I PLANT MY fists on the vanity and stare at my reflection in the mirror. I've been in here for seven minutes. I put the timer on as soon as I locked the door so I wouldn't take too long because I'm one-hundred percent psyching myself up to unlock that door and face the hot guy who is either throwing out amazing lines or who really does seem to think fate is the reason our paths crossed today.

It's hard to argue with the whole destiny thing, considering he's right—we've been at the same events before. I remember seeing him and wondering what the heck a surfer was doing at a gala. I also remember thinking he was hot, and not at all my type.

Except now that I've gotten to know him, I think he actually might be my type. And not at all like the jerks I typically end up with.

In which case I want to look like I care, but not too much. I adjust the top of my sleep tank, rinse once more with mouthwash, debate whether or not I want to toss a coin to help me decide whether or not I'm going to make the first move, and then I remember I used all my coins in the vending machine.

I smooth my hair one last time before I open the bathroom door. "Bathroom's all yours."

Lawson is standing by the table organizing our 7-Eleven purchases. He glances my way and his gaze drops from my face to my feet and then slowly comes back up. "Yes, it is." He gives his head a shake. "I mean, great. Thanks."

Shit, this is awkward.

Once he's in the bathroom, I head for the tent and get into bed so we can avoid more weirdness. I lie there for a while—it seems like an eternity—before the bathroom door creaks open, followed by the thwap-swoosh of Lawson's flip-flops as he approaches the tent.

The room goes mostly dark, aside from the dim glow coming from the direction of the bathroom. The flap opens and Lawson ducks inside. For a moment I consider pretending I'm asleep, but decide that's ridiculous. No one falls asleep that fast.

Lawson lies on his back and pulls the sheets all the way up to his chin. His arms go to his sides over the covers. "G'night," he says to the tent ceiling.

"Uh, g'night?"

I glance at him out of the corner of my eye—I'm also lying on my back, like a corpse. His eyes are closed. Maybe he doesn't want to make the first move? Or he doesn't want to assume I'm interested? I figured our discussion at the bar should be a fairly solid indicator that I am. I don't think his eyes have been closed for more than thirty seconds and I swear a low level snore comes out of him.

I hold my breath, sure I must be hearing things. "Lawson?"

I get nothing.

I prop myself up on my arm, the air mattress dipping, and peer at his face. His hair is still pulled up in a topknot. There's not much in the way of light filtering in, but I can clearly see that his eyes are closed. Another slightly louder snore escapes.

I poke him on the shoulder. "Hey."

His eyes pop open and he grins.

"You jerk! I thought you'd seriously fallen asleep in less than a minute! By your account it's supposed to be our fourth freaking date and you haven't even kissed me goodnight!"

His eyes search my face and his smile softens. "We've kind of jumped a whole bunch of dating hurdles in one day. I didn't want to make any assumptions. Plus, if you think I'm a shitty kisser, I'm going to have to sleep on that gross mattress with the polyester comforter." He thumbs in the direction of the bed.

I nod slowly, considering that. "Hmm. I guess you better make it a good one then."

He blows out a breath. "Okay. Game on, Nevah." His expression turns serious as he cups my cheek in his warm hand and tugs, ever so gently, pulling me in closer. His full lips brush softly over mine. He tilts his head to the right, thumb sliding along the edge of my jaw. "With or without tongue?" he asks.

"Date four should definitely include tongue, and it should be long. My toes should curl and I'll want to invite you up to my apartment."

"Mmm. Want me to work up to that? Like dates two

and three goodnight kisses first, or just dive right in?"

I smile as the end of his nose brushes against mine. "Hmm, I guess dates two and three are going to be a little different, aren't they?"

He nods solemnly. "Oh yeah. Like date two is more of a lingering kiss." He presses his lips to mine, firmer this time, then pulls my bottom lip between his. "And by the end of date three, the anticipation is pretty much killing me, knowing that kiss is coming, but not wanting the date to end." This time he slants his mouth over mine and strokes inside on a low groan. I welcome the velvet caress of his tongue, that little steel ball firm against all the soft.

I sink into the kiss, warming from the inside as his fingers slide into my hair, thumb gliding back and forth along the edge of my jaw. When he finally pulls back, we're both breathing heavily.

"I like date three kisses."

"Same." His thumb sweeps across my bottom lip. "But date four kisses are even better." He shifts and I lie back on the pillow. The air mattress dips when his elbow sinks in and tips me back in his direction. We both laugh and then I sigh when his lips sweep along my neck and he whispers, "So sexy," in my ear before skimming my cheek.

The next kiss is explosive. Heat funnels through my veins and I grip his shoulders, hitching my leg over his hip. I want the weight of him over me. I want his hands and his mouth on my skin. We grope and kiss, making out in a way I haven't done since I was a teenager and everything was new.

"What are date number five kisses like? I think I'm ready for some of those." I run my hands down his back, grabbing his ass and pushing down as I roll my hips.

Lawson brushes my nipple through my sleep tank. "Date five kisses get a little friskier."

"I'm on board with friskier."

"We're so on the same page right now, aren't we? Kindred kissing souls is what we are." I help Lawson pull my tank over my head. He cups one breast in his hand, thumb sweeping over my nipple as his tongue glides down my neck. When his lips close over my nipple, I arch and gasp at the feel of that hot steel ball circling my sensitive skin.

I want to know how that feels between my thighs.

"That's probably a date number ten kind of thing. You wanna fast forward?"

I freeze and I'm sure my eyes are ridiculously wide. I can feel my face heating up. "I didn't mean to say that out loud."

Lawson grins and licks at my nipple. "Up to you whether you want to stay at kiss five level or skip over a few to get to the good stuff."

"If that's date number ten, what happens between six and nine?"

His grin widens.

I laugh and roll my eyes. "Oh my God, sixty-nine. I walked right into that, didn't I?"

"You totally did." His hand glides down my stomach and his fingers flirt at the waist of my shorts, the pinkie slipping under the waistband. He pauses, though, his expression earnest. "Up a level or stay where we are?"

I reach up to tuck a loose tendril of hair behind his ear. I like the way he asks before he moves forward, never assuming. "I like you."

He kisses the end of my nose. "I like you, too. That's

why we're dating now."

I wrap my hand around the back of his neck and say, "Up a level," then pull his mouth back to mine.

Fifteen minutes later, my shorts are lying on the tent floor and I find out just how awesome date ten activities are. That little steel ball circles my sensitive skin, his hot, wet tongue so soft in comparison. I roll my hips and grip his hair, riding the wave of orgasm bliss.

Lawson settles between my hips and I feel the thick shaft against me through his shorts. "What date are we at now?"

"Whatever one you want." He kisses up the side of my neck.

"How about the one where I get to feel you inside me?"

He stills and pushes up on his forearms, eyes searching my face like maybe he's trying to see inside me. "We have all weekend if you'd rather press pause."

"Do you want to press pause?" Based on the way he keeps rolling his hips, I'm pretty sure I already know the answer.

His eyes fall closed for a second. "No, I don't."

"Me either."

"Condoms aren't in the tent. They're in my wallet." He rolls off the air mattress and lands on the floor with an oomph. "Be right back."

He's gone less than thirty seconds before he stumbles back into the tent. I help him out of his shorts and watch in fascination as he stretches the latex over the piercing and rolls it down his length. I can't imagine how much it had to hurt to get that. I'm guessing the pros must outweigh the cons, though.

I run my hand over the sheets. "Should we pick a

position?"

Lawson arches a brow. "Are you crazy? These are like date twenty-five through fifty positions. Let's start with the basics and work our way up to contortionist, yeah? And I think I might need to do some serious stretches and yoga before I even attempt this one." He points to the one by my right hip, then taps my knee. "Permission to ride this ride?"

"Permission granted," I say with a chuckle and part my legs.

He settles between them, stretching out over me. Every time he rests a forearm on the air mattress we tip to the side. He reaches between us and strokes the head over my clit, easing lower. He pushes in slowly and I moan at the feeling of being filled.

It's been a long time since I've been with anyone, and I don't remember the last time sex was this fun, or intense. Lawson moves slowly at first, giving me time to adjust. With each stroke I feel that piercing sliding deliciously along that perfect spot inside me, pushing me higher, taking me to the precipice and tipping me right over the edge.

He follows right after and we lie there, a tangle of limbs, breathing heavily as we come down from the high.

Lawson eventually rolls to the side and sprawls out beside me. "So freaking glad we didn't press pause."

"So much same." I lie there, basking in the glory of orgasm ecstasy.

"C'mere." He slides his arm under me and pulls me closer.

I pull the sheets up and rest my head on his chest. "That was fun."

"It really was." He kisses my forehead and drags his

fingers lightly up and down my arm. "Do you have your own room for the weekend?"

"I think Cosy reserved a yurt for me." I prop my chin on his pec. "Do you want to yurt with me tomorrow night?"

"That sounds like a messed-up sex position." He points to the one currently situated over his crotch. "This one, in fact."

I grin. "So that's a yes, then?"

"That's absolutely a yes."

Want to learn more about the Dude in Distress characters? Check out The Shacking Up Series
helenahunting.com/series/shacking-up

New York Times Bestselling Author

HELENA HUNTING

NYT and USA Today bestselling author of PUCKED, Helena Hunting lives on the outskirts of Toronto with her incredibly tolerant family and two moderately intolerant cats. She writes contemporary romance ranging from new adult angst to romantic sports comedy.

FIND MORE BOOKS BY HELENA HUNTING

BY VISITING HELENAHUNTING.COM

OTHER TITLES BY HELENA HUNTING

All IN SERIES

A Lie for a Lie

A Favor for a Favor

A Secret for a Secret

PUCKED SERIES

Pucked (Pucked #1)

Pucked Up (Pucked #2)

Pucked Over (Pucked #3)

Forever Pucked (Pucked Book #4)

Pucked Under (Pucked #5)

Pucked Off (Pucked #6)

Pucked Love (Pucked #7)

AREA 51: Deleted Scenes & Outtakes

Get Inked

Pucks & Penalties

SHACKING UP SERIES

Shacking Up

Getting Down (Novella)

Hooking Up

I Flipping Love You

Making Up

Handle With Care

THE CLIPPED WINGS SERIES

Cupcakes and Ink

Clipped Wings

Between the Cracks

Inked Armor

Cracks in the Armor

Fractures in Ink

STANDALONE NOVELS

The Librarian Principle

Felony Ever After

When Sparks Fly

Little Lies (writing As H. Hunting)

FOREVER ROMANCE STANDALONES

The Good Luck Charm

Meet Cute

Kiss My Cupcake

Made in United States
North Haven, CT
22 February 2023

32962400R00039